Wherever you go... I go.

This edition published by Parragon Books Ltd in 2015

Parragon Books Ltd
Chartist House
15–17 Trim Street
Bath BA1 1HA, UK
www.parragon.com

ISBN 978-1-4723-5922-3

Printed in China

Wherever you go... I go.

PaRragon

Bath • New York • Cologne • Melbourne • Delhi
Hong Kong • Shenzhen • Singapore • Amsterdam

The sun comes up and smiles on us
And starts to warm the early day.

My sleepy eyes can see you move.

Wherever you go... I go.

Then out we dash, to leap and play
And scramble in the morning sun.

You push some leaves
aside for me...

(Hey Mum! Hey, look!
Guess who's a tree?!)

Let's go have fun, and mess about.

Whenever you play...
I play.

(Oh no!)

The skies turn grey,
It starts to rain
And you just want to keep me dry...

(Thanks Mum!)

I run and shelter under you.

Wherever you are... I am.

And as we walk on, trunk in trunk
And talk about the things I'll do...

(You'll teach me, Mum...
you always do.)

You tell me just how much you care,

("I love you Mum," I sing to you!)

Whatever you love... I love.

Then when it's time to scrub me clean,
We'll splish and splosh and splash about.

You wash away my bathtime fears,

(Just don't forget behind my ears!)

Whenever you smile... I smile.

And when the day has reached its end
And both of us are getting tired,

I'll snuggle up and feel your warmth.
Whenever you sleep... I sleep.